KU-793-127

Gabriel

Dirty Bertie

my JOKE BOOK

April 4th
2011

From
Uncle Ed & family

STRIPES PUBLISHING
An imprint of Magi Publications
1 The Coda Centre, 189 Munster Road,
London SW6 6AW

A paperback original
First published in Great Britain in 2007

Characters created by David Roberts
Text copyright © Amanda Li, 2007
Illustrations copyright © David Roberts, 2007
With additional text by Alan MacDonald

ISBN-13: 978-1-84715-029-5

Printed and bound in Belgium by Proost

10 9 8 7 6 5 4 3 2

DAVID ROBERTS COMPILED BY AMANDA LI

Dirty Bertie

my JOKE BOOK

stripes

I've always wanted to write my own joke book. And here it is! All the jokes were collected by me and written on my hand or bits of paper (which is why some of them got a bit messy).

Some of the jokes I got from my friends, some are my family's and some I made up myself - the funniest ones. The rude jokes come at the end. And also the beginning and the middle (but don't tell Mum because she told me to leave them out).

There are some old jokes too - which is Gran's fault because all her jokes come from the Stone Age.

Take this book into school to amuse your friends and annoy your teachers. I hope it makes you laugh so much you get some stuff coming out of your nose.

Your friend,

Dirty Bertie

PS know-All Nick's joke is on page 204.
PPS Ha ha!

There once was a young boy called Bertie,
Whose ears were incredibly dirty,
When Mum came to look,
For potatoes to cook,
Behind Bertie's ears she found thirty!

Dirty Bertie
Joke Book

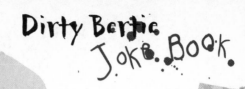

Dirty Bertie
Joke Book.

How many times did Bertie parp during class today?
Just a phew.

What part did Bertie get in the school play?
Peter Pong.

Bertie, can you break wind softly?

It's a breeze.

Dirty Bertie
Joke Book

What do you get when Bertie
blows off in the woods?

The wind in the willows.

Mum: Why are you taking so long
in the toilet, Bertie?

Bertie: I'm writing a poo-em.

Where does Bertie go to the
loo when he's camping?
In a tee-pee.

Dirty Bertie
Joke Book

Why should you leave Bertie's trainers well alone?

They're not to be sniffed at.

What's the difference between Bertie and a muddy young goat?

None, they're both dirty kids.

How did the toilet feel after Dirty Bertie came out?
A little flushed.

Dirty Bertie
Joke Book

What happened when Bertie crawled
under a cow?
He got a pat on the head.

What are Dirty Bertie's favourite clothes?
Dung-arees.

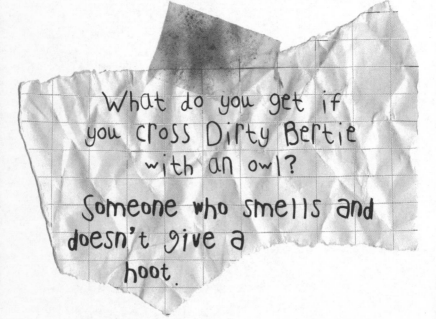

What do you get if
you cross Dirty Bertie
with an owl?

Someone who smells and
doesn't give a
hoot.

Dirty Bertie
Joke Book

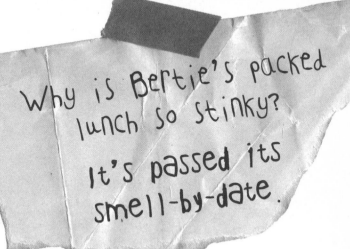

Why is Bertie's packed lunch so stinky?

It's passed its smell-by-date.

What does Bertie like doing
best after school?
Watching smell-i-vision.

Has anyone seen Dirty
Bertie's pants?
**No, but we've just got
wind of them.**

What's the only poo that doesn't smell?

I don't know.

Shampoo!

Know-All Nick: You know, Bertie, you should be a weather forecaster when you grow up.
Bertie: Why's that?
Know-All Nick: Cos you're an expert on wind.

Bertie's Top Ten Stinky Jokes

1. Why did the toilet paper
   roll down the hill?
   To get to the bottom.

2. What do you get if you cross a
   birthday cake and a tin of baked beans?
   A cake that blows out its own candles.

Dirty Bertie Joke Book

3. What do you call a very windy dinosaur?
A Stinkosaurus.

4. Where do very windy dinosaurs live?
Jurassic Parp.

5. Who's the smelliest ape in the world?
King Pong.

6. What flies through the air and stinks?
A smellicopter.

7. What do you call a fairy who smells?
Stinkerbell.

8. What did the skunk say when the
wind changed direction?
"It's all coming back to me now!"

9. What kind of fur do you get
from a skunk?
As fur away as possible.

10. Why do giraffes have very long necks?
Because their feet are so stinky.

Eugene: I think I know a joke about something really smelly.

Bertie: Go on, then.

Eugene: I'm trying to stink of it!

MY PET WHIFFER!

This bit's about dogs. My dog Whiffer's the best dog in the world. I wouldn't mind being a dog myself - all you do is eat, sleep, chase cats and wee against trees. Brilliant!

Dirty Bertie
Joke Book

How do you get Whiffer
to run a race?
Shout "One, Two, Flea, Go!"

How did Whiffer get all those
fleas on him?
They itch-hiked.

What happens when Whiffer's
fleas get angry?
They get hopping mad.

Dirty Bertie Joke Book

Does Whiffer get confused easily?
Yes, he's always barking up the wrong flea.

What did one of Whiffer's fleas say to
another of his fleas?
"Shall we walk or shall we take the dog?"

What did Whiffer say to his bone?
"It's been nice gnawing you."

What did Whiffer say when he
sat on some sandpaper?
"Ruff."

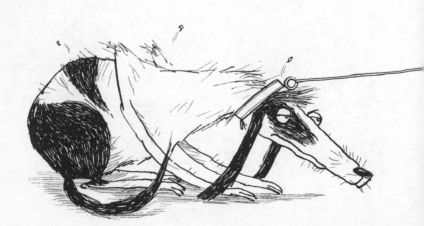

Dirty Bertie
Joke Book

What do you get when
Whiffer sits under a tree?
Bark.

Why is Whiffer like a rainstorm?
They both make lots of puddles.

How do you stop Whiffer from breaking
wind in the back seat of the car?
Put him in the front seat.

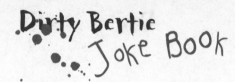

Where do fleas go in the winter?

Bertie's
Top Ten
Dog Jokes

1. What sort of
dog has no tail?
A hot dog.

Dirty Bertie
Joke Book

2. What sort of dog is good at looking after children?
A baby setter.

3. Have you got any dogs going cheap?
No, all mine go "Woof".

4. Why did the dog cross the road?
To find a barking space.

5. What do you call a group of very boring spotty dogs?
101 Dull-mations.

6. What do you get if you cross a dog with a hen?
Pooched eggs.

7. What kind of dog is always in a hurry?
A dash-hound.

8. What sort of stories do dogs like?
Furry tales.

9. What happens when it rains cats and dogs?

You might step in a poodle.

Eugene: I once heard a really good joke about a dog!

Bertie: I'm waiting...

Eugene: I've fur-gotten it.

SchoOL AND StUFF!

There are three things I like about school - playtime, lunchtime and going home! You can tell some of these jokes to your teachers.

Dirty Bertie Joke Book

How does Miss Boot guess what's
going on in Bertie's head?
She knows what he's stinking.

Dirty Bertie
Joke Book

Why has Miss Boot
gone cross-eyed?
She can't control her pupils.

What do you get if you meet
Mr Grouch on a dark night?
The school scaretaker.

Bertie: Miss, would you punish someone
for something they hadn't done?
Miss Boot: Of course not.
Bertie: Oh good – I haven't done
my homework.

Miss Boot: Bertie, why are you
eating your homework?
Bertie: You said it was a piece of cake.

What is Dirty Bertie doing
in the school library?
Looking for bookworms.

Miss Boot: Bertie, what is
easy to get into, but difficult to
get out of ?
Bertie: Trouble.

Why did Dirty Bertie spread
glue on his head?
**He thought it would help
things stick in his mind.**

Bertie's Top
Ten School
Jokes

1. What's the difference
between a school dinner
and a pile of poo?
**A school dinner comes
on a plate.**

Dirty Bertie
Joke Book

2. Why are school chips like a history lesson?
Because you get to discover ancient grease.

3. Why did the teacher turn all the lights on?
Because her class was so dim.

Name two days of the week that start with 'T'.

Today and Tomorrow.

5. What do ghost teachers
give their pupils to do?
Moanwork.

6. Why did the maths teacher
take a ruler to bed with him?
**He wanted to see how long
he would sleep.**

7. **Pupil:** Teacher, teacher, my pen's run out.
Teacher: Well, go and chase after it then.

8. Have you heard the one about the pupil
who only had a bath once a year?
He was in a class of his own.

9. What is a maths teacher's
favourite creature?
An adder.

10. What is a history teacher's favourite fruit?
Dates.

Bertie: Eugene, didn't you know the school bell's gone?

Eugene: Oh no, who stole it?

MiND YOUR MANNERS!

"Don't slurp! Don't burp! Elbows off the table!" If I was king I'd pass a law that everyone has to have BAD manners. Just think of it - all those teachers picking their noses. - ugh!

Dirty Bertie
Joke Book

Mum: Bertie, don't put your fingers
in the soup!
Bertie: It's all right Mum, it isn't hot.

Why is Bertie eating his dinner
with a spade?
He likes to shovel it down.

How does Whiffer eat his dinner?
He wolfs it down.

Why has Dirty Bertie got holes in his
underpants?
So he can get his feet through them!

Mum: Bertie, why do you keep
scratching yourself?
Bertie: No one else knows where I itch.

Dad: Bertie, why are you staring at the
alphabet?
Bertie: I'm minding my Ps and Qs.

Dirty Bertie
Joke Book

How does Bertie eat a turkey dinner?
He just gobbles it down.

Why is Bertie eating his lunch
like a football match?
There's a lot of dribbling.

What does Bertie
say at parties?
"Happy Burp-day!"

Dirty Bertie
Joke Book

Bertie: What do you get if you wiggle
your fingers in a glass of milk?
Eugene: I don't know.
Bertie: A handshake.

Bertie: What's yellow, brown and hairy?
Eugene: I don't know.
Bertie: Cheese on toast on the carpet.

What happened when Bertie
burped in front of
the Queen?
She gave him a
Royal pardon.

Bertie's
Top Ten Not
Very Polite
Jokes

1. What lies on your plate
and tells you to shut up?
Rude food.

Dirty Bertie Joke Book

2. What do you get if you wipe
your nose on the arms of your jumper?
Greensleeves.

3. What do you call a reindeer who
won't say please and thank you?
Rude-olph.

4. What did the father ghost say
to the baby ghost?
"Only spook when you're spooken to!"

5. What did the mummy monster
say to the little monster?
"Don't talk with someone in your mouth!"

6. Who shouted "Knickers!" at the big bad wolf?
Little Rude Riding Hood.

7. Which queen always burped
at the dinner table?
Queen Hic-toria.

8. Which king used to blow off
at the dinner table?
Richard the Lionfart.

9. What colour is a burp?
Burple.

10. What's the best thing to
put in a birthday cake?
Your teeth.

Eugene: I know a joke about a funny taste.

Bertie: What's that?

Eugene: It's on the tip of my tongue.

CREEPY CRAWLIES!

Worms, slugs, flies, snails - they all make brilliant pets. I like to bring them inside and make them feel at home, but my family doesn't seem to appreciate my collection of creepy crawlies.

Suzy: Bertie, what's this fly doing in my soup?
Bertie: The front crawl, I think.

How did Bertie create his flea circus?
He started from scratch.

Dirty Bertie
Joke Book

What happened to Bertie's flea circus?
Whiffer came along and stole the show.

Where did Bertie take the sick wasp?
To the waspital.

Why can't Bertie trust his pet worm?
He always wriggles out of everything.

Dirty Bertie
Joke Book

Suzy: Bertie, are you giving
those nits breakfast?
Bertie: It's just a bowl of
lice krispies.

Suzy: Bertie, there are fleas
running down your arm!
Bertie: They're having a
flea-legged race.

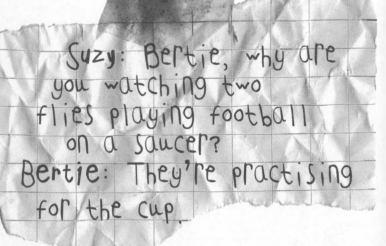

Suzy: Bertie, why are
you watching two
flies playing football
on a saucer?
Bertie: They're practising
for the cup.

Dirty Bertie
Joke Book

Suzy: Bertie, why is there an insect standing guard outside your bedroom door?
Bertie: Oh, that's my sentry-pede.

Suzy: Bertie, why have you named your lizard 'Tiny'?
Bertie: Because he's my newt.

Bertie, why have you put a frog in my bed?

Well, I couldn't find a worm!

Dirty Bertie
Joke Book

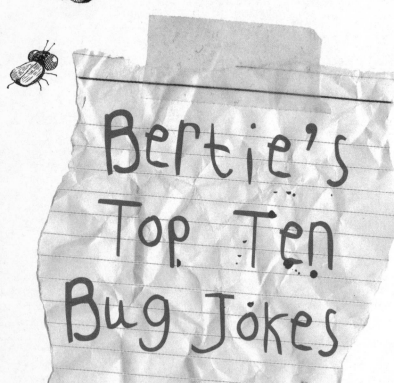

Bertie's
Top Ten
Bug Jokes

50

Dirty Bertie
Joke Book

1. What do you call a very stupid head louse?
A nitwit.

2. What's the definition of a slug?
A homeless snail.

3. What's the definition of a caterpillar?
A worm in a fur coat.

4. What do you call an evil flying insect?
A Baddy Long Legs.

5. What did the firefly say when
he flew to the loo?
"When you gotta glow, you gotta glow."

6. Why is the letter 't' important
to a stick insect?
**Because without it, he'd
be a sick insect.**

Dirty Bertie
Joke Book

7. What did the spider say when
its web broke?
"Darn it!"

8. What do earwigs sing at football matches?
"Earwig-go, earwig-go, earwig-go!"

9. What do you call a bee
who is always complaining?
A grumble bee.

10. Why did the fly fly?
Because the spider spied 'er.

Dirty Bertie
Joke Book

Eugene: I know a good insect joke.

Bertie: Can you remember it this time?

Eugene: No, and it's really bugging me.

What's the difference between
a bogey and a green bean?
Bertie doesn't eat green beans.

What did Bertie's nose say to him?
"Stop picking on me!"

What are Bertie's favourite crisps?
Sneeze and onion flavour.

Is it possible to stop Dirty Bertie
from smelling?
Yes – hold his nose.

Why do apples on trees remind
Bertie of bogeys?
They're fresh, green and ready to pick.

Why did Dirty Bertie stick his head
out of the car window?
So the wind would blow his nose.

Dirty Bertie Joke Book

What do you get if you cross Whiffer with Bertie's nose?

A sniffer dog.

Dirty Bertie
Joke Book

What do you get if you cross Bertie's
nose with a bag of sweets?
Pick'n'mix.

What did Bertie's nose say to
Bertie's hanky?
"Well, blow me!"

Bertie, you must have
been made upside-down?

How do you
know that?

Cos your nose
runs and your
feet smell!

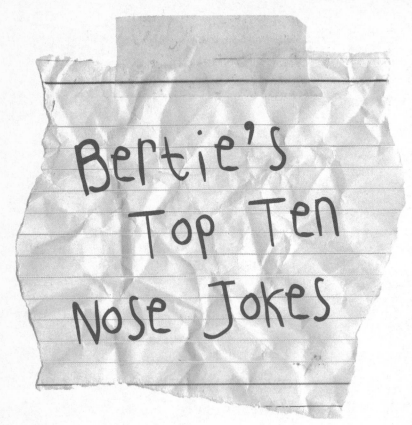

Bertie's
Top Ten

Nose Jokes

1. Who is the boss of
the hankies?
The handker-chief!

Dirty Bertie
Joke Book

2. What's big, scary and gets up your nose?
The Bogey Man.

3. What did one ear say to the other ear?
"There's something between us that smells."

4. Why were the nose and handkerchief always fighting?
They couldn't meet without coming to blows.

5. Knock, knock.
Who's there?
Snot.
Snot who?
'Snot fair!

6. What did the nose shout at the auditions
for the school play?
"Pick me, pick me!"

7. **Knock, knock.**
Who's there?
Nose.
Nose who?
Nose anyone with a tissue?

8. What's green and hangs off trees?
Giraffe snot.

9. Why do gorillas have such big noses?
Well, have you seen the size of their fingers?

10. What did one nose sing to another nose?
"For sneeze a jolly good fellow!"

Eugene: I think I know a joke about a runny nose.

Bertie: Get on with it then.

Eugene: Oh no – I've blown it again.

WHAT A LOAD OF RUBBISH!

I love rubbish! You can find all sorts of interesting things if you poke about in a dustbin. Here are my rubbish jokes. Ha ha!

What did Whiffer say when
the dustcart ran over his tail?

**It won't be
long now.**

Where's Bertie taking all that rubbish
on his bike?
He's recycling it.

Dirty Bertie
Joke Book

What pet insect does Bertie keep in his bin?
His litter bug.

Dustman: There are ten flies on that dustbin.
If I swat one of them, how many will be left?
Bertie: Just the dead one!

Mum: Bertie, why are you carrying stinking
heaps of rubbish into your bedroom?
Bertie: Because you said my room was a
dump!

Knock, knock.
Who's there?
Bin.
Bin who?
Bin anywhere nice for your holidays?

What happened to the dustman who
complained that he hadn't got anything
to put the rubbish in?
He got the sack.

Dirty Bertie Joke Book

Miss Skinner: Bertie, what do you want to be
when you're older?
Bertie: A rubbish collector.
Miss Skinner: But you haven't got any
experience.
Bertie: Don't worry, I'll pick it up as I go along.

When I grow up
I want to drive
a dustcart.

Well, I won't
stand in
your way!

Bertie's Top Ten Dustmen Jokes

1. Why did the dustman marry the cleaner?
She swept him off his feet.

Dirty Bertie
Joke Book

2. **First dustcart driver:** Are my indicators
working?
Second dustcart driver: Yes, no,
yes, no, yes, no.

3. Why do dustmen never accept invitations?
Because they are refuse men.

4. Why are dustmen dirty?
Because they lead a life of grime.

5. Did you hear the one about the empty
rubbish bin?
There's nothing in it.

6. Why was the dustman only wearing
one glove?
**The weather forecast said on the one
hand it might be hot and on the
other hand it might be cold.**

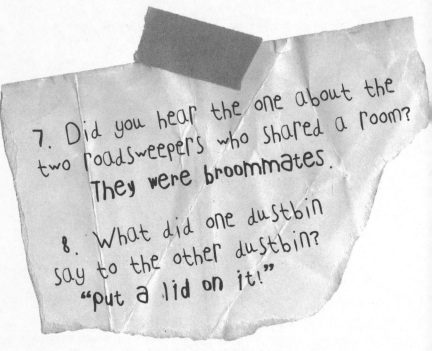

7. Did you hear the one about the two roadsweepers who shared a room?
They were broommates.

8. What did one dustbin say to the other dustbin?
"Put a lid on it!"

9. Why was the roadcleaner shampooing his broom?
He wanted a clean sweep.

10. What is a dustman's favourite dance?
The can-can.

Eugene: I know a joke about a heap of litter.

Bertie: So tell me!

Eugene: It was such a load of rubbish, I couldn't repeat it.

MY FAMILY!

My mum and dad tell me off about a billion times a day. Sometimes, Mum tells me off when I haven't done anything! She says she's saving time.

Dirty Bertie
Joke Book

What do you call two people who
embarrass you in front of your friends?
Mum and Dad!

Mum: Bertie, why have you got
a mouse in your bath?
Bertie: You said I had to get squeaky clean.

Dad: Bertie, stop picking bogeys and
putting them in your mouth!
Bertie: Well, you told me to eat
my greens.

Dad: Bertie, what would you like
to be when you grow up?
Bertie: Filthy rich!

Mum: Bertie, every time you are
naughty I get another grey hair.
Bertie: Mum, you must have been really
naughty when you were a child. Look at
Gran's hair!

Dirty Bertie
Joke Book

Bertie: Gran, your tights are all wrinkled!
Gran: I'm not wearing any.

Mum: Bertie, I told you to put a clean
pair of socks on every day.
Bertie: Yes, but now it's the end of the
week and I can't get my shoes on!

Suzy: What do you mean by telling
everyone I'm an idiot?
Bertie: Sorry, I didn't know it was
meant to be a secret.

Suzy: If you eat any more ice
cream you'll burst.
Bertie: OK, pass the ice cream
and duck.

Why are Bertie's gran's false teeth like stars?
Because they come out at night.

Dirty Bertie
Joke Book

Suzy: Where are you going?
Bertie: To the cinema.
Suzy: What, with dirt all over your face?
Bertie: No, with Eugene!

Bertie: Gran, why do you cover up your
mouth when you sneeze?
Gran: So I can catch my false teeth.

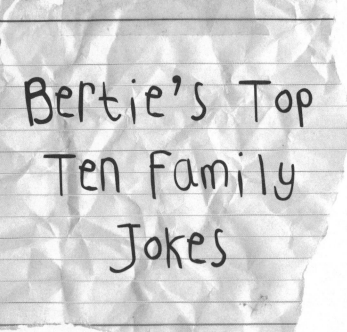

Bertie's Top
Ten Family
Jokes

1. What do you call a very
small parent?
A mini-mum.

Dirty Bertie Joke Book

2. What do ghosts call their mums and dads?
Trans-parents.

3. Where do monsters drop their kids off
when they're working?
Child scare centres.

4. Why were the ancient Egyptians confused?
Because their daddies were mummies.

5. What did the mother broom say
to the baby broom?
"Go to sweep."

6. Why was the biscuit crying?
**Because his mother had been
a wafer so long.**

7. Why was the little ant confused?
Because all his uncles were ants.

8. Why was the baby strawberry crying?
His parents were in a jam.

9. What do you call a cannibal who
eats his mother's sisters?
An aunt-eater.

10. Knock, knock.
Who's there?
Granny.
Knock, knock.
Who's there?
Granny.
Knock, knock.
Who's there?
Granny.
Knock knock.
Who's there?
Aunt.
Aunt who?
**Aunt you glad I got rid
of all those grannies?**

Eugene: I was going to tell you a great joke about my family but I've changed my mind.

Bertie: Good, does the new one work any better?

Dirty Bertie
Joke Book

Will the person who took my ladder
return it to me immediately.
Otherwise steps will be taken.

Mr Grouch - Caretaker

That means
you, Bertie.

Dirty Bertie
Joke Book

That's all for now!

Heads and shoulders, cheesy toes, cheesy toes,

Heads and shoulders, cheesy toes, cheesy toes,

Eyes and ears and a finger up your nose,

Heads and shoulders, cheesy toes, cheesy toes.

Dirty Bertie
Joke Book

Write your own jokes here.